THE GREEN CAT

THE
GREEN CAT

Story and illustrations by
Robert Jacobson

LONGFEATHER PRESS

ISBNs
hardback: 978-0-9838668-3-1
paperback: 978-0-9838668-4-8
ebook: 978-0-9838668-5-5

Book design by Robert Jacobson with technical assistance by Erik Jacobson at LongfeatherBookDesign.com.

Longfeather Press
2048 Arborcrest Road
Moscow, ID 83843

GreenCatBook.com

Harmony: playing beautifully together

HELLO, HELLO.
 Please say **hello**
  to me, the big green cat.
I've come to make
  my home with you.
   It's true. How cool is that?

I know you weren't
   expecting me.
    So what a nice surprise!
Already you're
   in love with me.
    I see it in your eyes.

Now let me tell
   you what I need
    to make myself at home—
I'd like a bedroom
   with tv,
    and my own telephone.

I also need
  a place to scratch,
  a place to shed my hair.
But never mind,
  I'm sure I'll find
  some curtains or a chair.

And here's a list
  of things I eat.
  (I like to eat a lot.)
Please serve it in
  a fancy bowl,
  the best one that you've got.

There's more … but that's
enough for now.
It's time for me to rest.
A catnap would
be wonderful.
It's what I do the best.

ice cream
catfish
munchies
chicken
gravy
bugs
ss

I have a long
  and restful sleep.
  But then, a noise I hear.
A kitten's standing
  on my face.
  She's shouting in my ear.

WAKE UP! WAKE UP!
  she yells at me.
  You big green lazy **jerk.**
All you do is
  eat and sleep
  while we do all the **work!**

Did she say work?
  I ask myself.
  What kind of word is that?
It's not a word
  I like to hear.
  Don't say it to a cat!

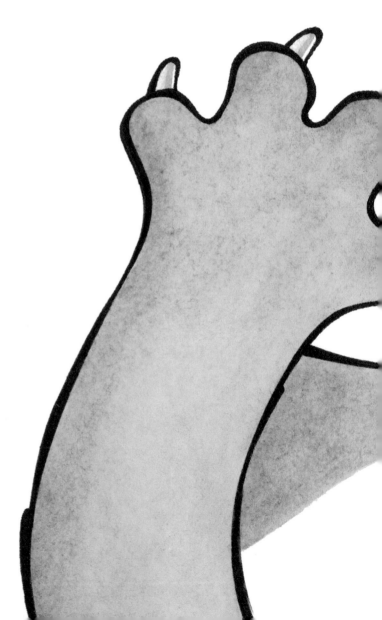

Besides, you call
   that **work**? I say.
   To run around the floor?
To catch a bug?
   To chase a string?
   That's **play**. And nothing more.

That stuff we do
   makes people laugh,
   the kitten says to me.
That's how we earn
   our food, you know.
   The food here isn't free.

Oh, that's not true,
  I say to her.
For cats, **all** things are free.
And we don't do
  a lick of work,
  as everyone can see.

We still get tired,
   the kitten whines.
   And you don't do a thing.
Now we want **you**
   to play with us.
   We're bored with bugs and string.

Okay. Okay.
   I guess I can.
   I know a trick or two.
Forget about
   that kitten stuff.
   I'll show you something new.

We walk to the
   piano then.
   I hop up on the keys.
I'll show you how
   to play this thing.
   So pay attention, please.

Can you see how
  I'm standing here?
  Up on my tippy toes?
My front feet play
  the high notes, see?
  My back feet play the lows.

Some notes are very
  hard to reach.
  That doesn't make me fail.
I stretch way out,
  a lo-o-o-ng way out,
  and play them with my tail.

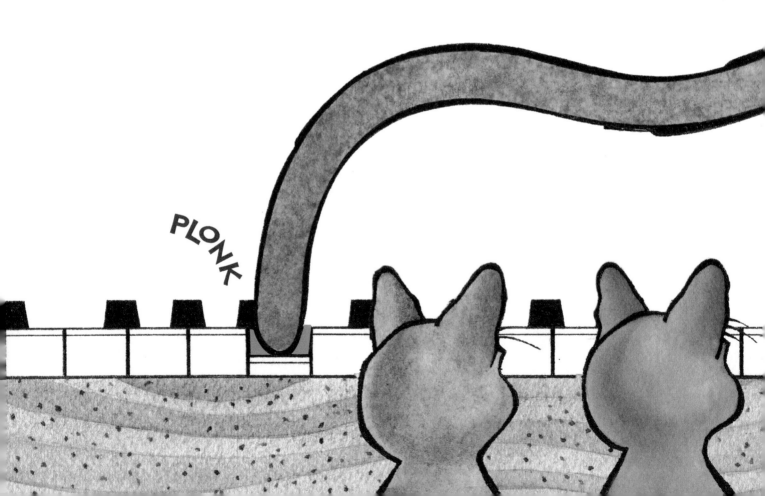

PLONK

And while I play
  some rock and roll,
  I hear one kitten say,
Oh, that's so cool,
  it's **more** than cool.
  This dude can really play!

The kittens laugh
  and sway and dance,
  those crazy little nuts.
It's fun to watch
  the way they move,
  and wave their little butts.

All right, I say.
  Come on, you guys.
  Jump up here on the keys.
Let's play a song
  together now,
  and make some harmonies.

But these guys don't
  do harmonies.
  They both just bounce around.
They hop and flip
  and howl and yip
  and make an awful sound.

But still it's kind
   of fun, you know,
   to bang away so loud.
We keep it up
   'til finally
   our music draws a crowd.

A fist starts pounding
   on the door.
   We hear some people shout,
Get down from there,
   you rotten cats!
Get down! **Get down! GET OUT!**

It's time to go,
    my friends, I say.
    And I mean **GO.** Right **NOW!**
No time to finish
    up our song.
    No time to take a bow.

So down we jump,
   and off we run.
   We leave that fuss behind.
We find a perfect
   hiding place
   that no one else can find.

We settle down
   and catch our breath.
   We're happy as can be.
When everything
   is quiet, then
   one kitten says to me,

Please pardon me
for asking, sir,
but why are you so green?
We've never seen
a cat like you,
if you know what I mean.

Well, let me ask
   you this, my friends,
   Why are **you** brown and gray?
You could be yellow,
   blue or pink.
   So what? That's what I say.

You just be proud
   that you're a cat.
   A cat of any kind.
We are the best
   of animals.
   You just keep that in mind.

Some folks don't like
   our music, kids.
   Who cares? Not you, not me.
We'll just make music
   for ourselves.
   We'll **PURRRRR** in harmony.

CPSIA information can be obtained
at www.ICGtesting.com
Printed in the USA
LVIC04n1403291115
464448LV00002B/15

* 9 7 8 0 9 8 3 8 6 6 8 4 8 *